ANYBODY HOME?

by Tracey West

interior illustrations by
Frank Mayo

STECK-VAUGHN
ELEMENTARY · SECONDARY · ADULT · LIBRARY

A Harcourt Company

www.steck-vaughn.com

Chapter · 1

———

The criminal struggled under Night Rover's iron grip.

"You're off the streets for good now!" Night Rover said.

"Rahji, I asked for a Health Hero. This is a Hero Hut Special," Hank Harris said. He held up a sandwich filled with cheese, salami, ham, lettuce, and tomato.

"Sorry, Hank," Rahji Singh said. He put down the new *Night Rover* comic book he was reading. "I guess I wasn't concentrating."

Hank rubbed his hand across his balding head. "You're lucky I'm such a nice boss," he said. "Just be more careful. We want to keep our customers happy." Hank turned and walked back into the kitchen.

"That was a close call, Rahji," Mike Pitski whispered. He picked up a rag and threw it to Rahji.

Rahji caught the rag and began wiping the counter in front of him. "You're right," he sighed. "I don't want to lose this job."

Rahji stashed his copy of *Night Rover* under the counter. He hated to put away the comic book. It was a great story. By day, Lalit Jain was an accountant. But by night, he was the Night Rover. Rahji liked the way Night Rover was able to catch criminals when the police didn't have a clue. He also thought it was cool that Night Rover was from India, like his own parents.

Rahji heard the bell ring on the door of the Hero Hut. A tall, young woman walked in.

Hank came out from the kitchen

carrying a white paper bag. "Hey, Jean," he called. "I've got your Health Hero right here."

Jean Lewin smiled. "Thanks, Hank," she said.

"How was your vacation?" Rahji asked his favorite customer.

"My vacation was great," answered Jean. Then the smile disappeared from her face. "But my house was broken into while I was away."

"No way!" Mike exclaimed.

Jean nodded her head. "I'm afraid so, Mike," she said. "And my place isn't the first house in Hogan Park that's been broken into."

"Hey, Rahji, Hogan Park's your neighborhood," Mike announced.

"Yeah," Rahji said. "And it's Hank's neighborhood, too," he added.

Hank handed Jean the paper bag. "This sandwich is on the house today," he said kindly.

Jean thanked Hank and left. Hank headed back into the kitchen.

"Man, I can't believe there's been another burglary," Mike said to Rahji.

"I wonder why the police haven't figured out who's doing this?" Rahji said. "I bet I could."

Mike laughed. "Rahji, you're pretty smart, but you're no Night Rover," he teased.

Just then the phone rang. "I'll get it," Hank called from the back.

A few minutes later Hank came up front. He looked shaken. Rahji could tell something was wrong.

"What's going on?" Rahji asked.

"That was the police on the phone," Hank said in a low voice. "My house has been broken into."

9

Chapter · 2

——

"Was your house robbed, too? No way!" Mike exclaimed.

Rahji turned to Hank. "Did they take a lot of stuff?" he asked.

"I don't know yet," Hank answered. "I've got to go to the house and talk to the police. My next-door neighbor saw my back door open and called them."

"Can we go with you?" Rahji asked. "We could help figure out what's going on."

"No thanks," Hank said. "Let's just lock up here."

About fifteen minutes later Hank, Rahji, and Mike stepped out into the hot July sun. Hank locked the door behind them.

"See you later, guys," Hank said.

Mike turned to Rahji. "So, what should we do now?" he asked.

Rahji looked down the street. "Let's go to the video arcade," he suggested. "I haven't played the new Night Rover game lately."

The arcade was only a few blocks away. The place was always noisy and crowded with kids during the summer. Rahji and Mike headed to the corner of the room. The Night Rover game was a giant black machine.

"We're in luck, Mike. No one's on it," Rahji said. He slid a quarter into the slot. "You want to go first?" Rahji asked his friend.

"No thanks, Rahji. You're the pro," said Mike.

Night Rover's theme music blared as the game started up. In Level One, Night Rover tackled five faceless thugs. Rahji used the buttons to throw punches and deliver hard kicks. Excellent! In a minute, he already had four down. He was about to complete the first round when he felt a tap on his shoulder.

"Quit it, Mike. I'm on a roll," Rahji grumbled.

"I'm not Mike. And you'd better quit playing. This is my machine," a voice answered.

Rahji turned away from the screen. Keith Ross, a kid who delivered papers in Rahji's neighborhood, was glaring at him.

Rahji turned back to the game. "I don't see your name anywhere on here," he said.

"Yeah, man, get lost," Mike added.

Suddenly Keith shoved Rahji. Rahji banged his elbow against the glass.

"I said, get off the game, man!" Keith yelled.

"Let's wait one more minute," Rahji whispered.

"What's going on?" Mike whispered back to his friend.

Rahji pointed to the door. Keith Ross had just walked in. He headed straight for the Night Rover video game.

"This is the exact same time he came

"I don't know, but you were right. He wasn't worth fighting," Rahji said. "Come on, Mike, let's go see how Hank's doing."

Hogan Park was a neighborhood on the edge of town. It was about twenty minutes away from the arcade.

When Mike and Rahji got to Hank's house, the door was open. They walked in. Hank was talking to a police officer.

"Hey, Mike. Hey, Rahji," Hank called.

"You boys know Officer Lopez, don't you?"

"Sure," Rahji answered. "I've made Hero Hut deliveries to your house. You live here in Hogan Park, too."

"That's right," smiled Officer Carmen Lopez. "We're neighbors."

"We want to help figure out this burglary thing," Rahji said.

Officer Lopez smiled. "We could use some help," she admitted. "These burglaries have been going on for three weeks, since the end of June. And we don't have many clues."

"I heard all the break-ins were in Hogan Park," said Rahji.

Officer Lopez hesitated. Then she nodded. "I guess I can tell you about it. It's been in the newspaper," she said. "The burglaries all happened during the day. The victims were either on vacation or at work, like Hank."

Something clicked in Rahji's head.

"Did you ever think the burglar might be a kid?" he asked.

"What makes you think so?" Officer Lopez asked.

"The burglaries began at the end of June. That's when school lets out. And they take place during the day. Lots of kids have nothing to do during the day in the summer, unless they have jobs," Rahji explained.

Officer Lopez nodded. "You might have something there, Rahji," she admitted. She pulled out a notebook and wrote something on it. "I'm giving

you my phone number at the station. If you come up with anything else, let me know," she told Rahji.

Hank walked with Officer Lopez to the front door. Rahji turned to Mike and smiled at him.

Mike shook his head. "You win, Rahji! It looks like Night Rover has come to Hogan Park!"

Chapter · 3

POW! CRUNCH! Rahji hit the buttons on the Night Rover video game. Each time Night Rover hit a criminal, Rahji imagined he was punching Keith Ross.

"Are we going to spend our whole day in this arcade?" Mike asked. "I thought you'd want to figure out who's doing those burglaries after what happened yesterday."

"I will," Rahji answered. "But I never got to finish yesterday's game."

Rahji kept pushing the buttons. He was already up to Level 20.

"I did it!" Rahji announced after another minute. "I made the top ten!"

A list of the top ten scorers came up

on the screen. The number six spot was blank. PLEASE ENTER YOUR NAME NOW, the screen said. Rahji entered his initials, RS.

"I wonder if Keith's name is here," Rahji said to Mike.

Rahji eyed the other names on the list. "Weird," he thought. "These names don't look like names at all." One read 21LARCH. Another read 5MAIN.

Something clicked in Rahji's mind. He scrolled down the list. "Mike, check this out! These aren't names. They're addresses!" Rahji exclaimed.

"What?" said Mike. He looked at the

list on the screen. "Hey, you're right. And look at the second one—13WILSON. That's Hank's address!"

The address in the number one slot was 33MAIN. "I'll be right back," Rahji said as he ran off. "I want to check something out."

Rahji returned a few minutes later. "I called Officer Lopez to see if there were any break-ins today," he explained. "She said one was just reported at 33 Main Street."

"That's the address in the number one slot! What do you think this means?" Mike asked.

"I'm not sure," Rahji said. "But it seems there's some connection between this Night Rover game and the burglaries. I think we should stake out the game," he added.

About three hours and six slices of pizza later, they were still waiting.

"Rahji, we've been hanging out here all day," Mike complained. "We haven't

seen any suspects yet. Maybe we should just give up."

Rahji sighed. "Maybe you're right," he said. "But I just can't believe . . ."

Rahji stopped talking and pushed Mike behind the nearest video game.

"No way!" Rahji yelled back. His elbow hurt. Maybe it was time to throw some punches at Keith.

Mike tugged Rahji's shoulder. "Hey, Rahji, look. You're twice as big as this little runt. He's just not worth it," Mike pointed out.

Rahji hesitated, but he knew Mike was right. "Okay," he agreed.

"I wonder what that guy's problem is," Mike said when they were outside.

in yesterday," Rahji whispered.

Rahji and Mike watched Keith work the game. It was easy to tell he was a real pro at it. About fifteen minutes went by before Keith's game ended and he added his name to the top ten list. Keith glanced around quickly. Then he left the arcade.

"Let's check out the list," Rahji said.

Rahji and Mike walked over to the game. The new top ten scorers list was flashing on the screen. Rahji's initials had moved down to the number seven spot. In the number one spot it said 21BIRCH.

Mike's mouth dropped open. "Rahji, that's your address!" he exclaimed.

Rahji gasped. "It looks like he's entering the addresses of the houses that are going to be hit next," he said. "I bet he's leaving a message for the burglars."

"But why would Keith pick your house?" asked Mike.

"My parents left town this morning for a week. I'm staying with Hank, remember?" Rahji said.

"Yeah, I remember," answered Mike. "But how did Keith know your parents were going away?"

"I don't know," said Rahji. "They didn't tell anybody except Hank and . . ." The thought hit Rahji like a lightning bolt. "And the newspaper delivery service!" he shouted.

Chapter · 4

"So Keith knew your parents would be away because he delivers your newspaper!" Mike exclaimed. "What are you going to do, Rahji?"

"I have an idea, but we've got to act fast," Rahji answered. He pulled a piece of paper from his pocket. He gave it to Mike. "I got Officer Lopez's number from the phone book. Call and tell her to expect the burglars at her doorstep soon."

Mike rushed out to find a phone. Rahji hurried over to the Night Rover video game. He knew what he had to do. Somehow he had to beat Keith's newest number one score. He remembered Officer Lopez's address from delivering for Hero Hut. Rahji would enter Officer Lopez's address in the number one slot. The crooks would go to her house instead of his.

Rahji took a deep breath. He was good at the Night Rover game, but he hadn't had as much practice as Keith. Could he beat Keith's score in just one shot? And could he do it fast enough?

Rahji slid a quarter into the machine. The Night Rover theme blared. At Level One, Rahji threw punch after punch. All five thugs vanished from the screen.

At Level Two these thugs were bigger and stronger. But Rahji polished them off easily.

From the corner of his eye Rahji saw Mike coming back. He didn't look up. He had to concentrate.

Level Eight. Level Nine. Sweat poured down his forehead. Would he make it in time?

Rahji was so into the game he almost

didn't realize when Level 20 was over.

"You did it, Rahji! You beat Keith's score!" Mike yelled.

"Excellent! But I'm not quite done yet," Rahji answered. He quickly entered 63JONES in the number one slot. If he was right, the crooks would go to 63 Jones Street—Officer Lopez's house.

Rahji glanced around the arcade. "We'd better get out of the way now," he said. "Let's leave this game—and let the *real* game begin!"

Rahji led Mike to a spot in the corner of the room. They didn't have long to wait. Soon two tough-looking guys walked into the arcade and headed straight to the Night Rover game. They looked at the screen. Then they ran out the door.

"Do you think they're the burglars?" Mike asked.

"I bet they are," Rahji said. "Let's get over to Officer Lopez's house now. I want to see what happens."

The two boys ran at Night Rover speed to Hogan Park.

When Rahji and Mike got to Officer Lopez's house a squad car was parked out front. Two officers were leading the guys from the arcade out to the car.

Officer Lopez was standing at the top of the steps. She was smiling.

"What happened?" Rahji asked.

"You should know," Officer Lopez laughed. Then she explained. "When I got Mike's phone call, I wasn't sure what to expect. I called the precinct for backup just in case. It wasn't long before our two friends here decided to jimmy the lock to my back door with a crowbar. They didn't know I was inside. I had them handcuffed before they knew what hit them."

Rahji felt great. But there was one thing still bothering him.

"Officer Lopez," Rahji said. "There's another guy involved in this, too. His name is Keith Ross."

Officer Lopez nodded. "We're looking for him now," she said. "These guys

ratted on him as soon as we read them their rights. They said Keith organized the whole thing. He told them which houses would be empty during the day."

"Way to go!" Mike shouted. "It looks like this case is closed," he added.

"Yeah, that was exciting," said Rahji. "But there's just one bad thing about all this detective work," Rahji complained. Then he grinned. "I haven't had any time to finish reading my new *Night Rover* comic book!"